Wishes really

Lucky Stars

Lucky Star that shines so bright,
Who will need your help tonight?
Light up the sky, it's thanks to you
Wishes really do come true . . .

Lucky Stars

Explore the sparkling world of the stars at
www.luckystarsbooks.co.uk

Wishes really do come true

Lucky Stars

The Christmas Wish

Phoebe Bright

Illustrated by Karen Donnelly

MACMILLAN CHILDREN'S BOOKS

A Working Partners book

Special thanks to Valerie Wilding

First published 2012 by Macmillan Children's Books
a division of Macmillan Publishers Limited
20 New Wharf Road, London N1 9RR
Basingstoke and Oxford
Associated companies throughout the world
www.panmacmillan.com

ISBN 978-1-4472-3613-9

A CIP catalogue record for this book is available from
the British Library.

Printed and bound by CPI Group (UK) Ltd, Croydon CR0 4YY

For Sue and Greg, who make Christmas happy

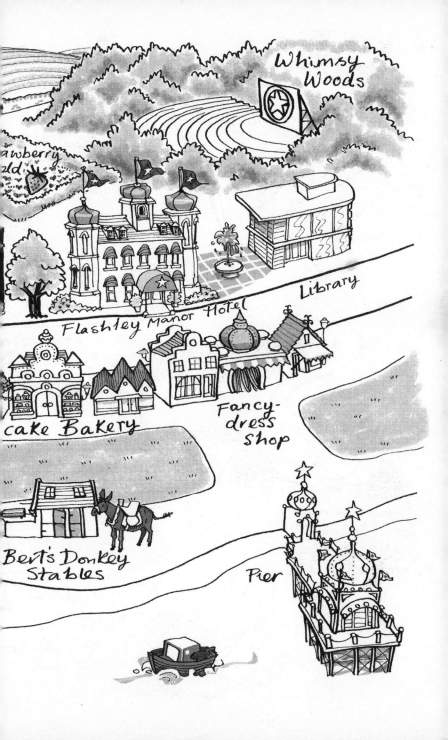

Contents

Hello, friend!

I'm Stella Starkeeper and I want to tell you a secret. Have you ever gazed up at the stars and thought how magical they looked? Well, you're right. Stars really do have magic!

Their precious glittering light allows me to fly down from the sky, all the way to Earth. You see, I'm always on the lookout for boys and girls who are especially kind and helpful. I train them to become Lucky Stars - people who can make wishes come true!

So the next time you're under the twinkling night sky, look out for me. I'll be floating among the stars somewhere. Do give me a wave!

Love from
Stella x

1
The Winter Star

'I'm so lucky to be able to fly!' cried Cassie.
She grinned in delight at Stella Starkeeper,
the young woman floating alongside her
through the night sky.

Stella wore a crown made of fine silver
strands that gleamed in the moonlight.
She was dressed all in silver, and her fair
hair flowed behind her like a shimmering
river. She whisked her star-tipped wand
in a spiral, and hundreds of tiny sparkles

showered around both of them.

Cassie was wearing her blue coat over her pyjamas. She laughed when she saw how pretty it looked now, as if it was sprinkled with tiny stars.

A sparkle on Cassie's wrist caught her eye. It was the charm bracelet Stella had given her at the beginning of summer, on her seventh birthday. Cassie had earned seven charms by helping to make wishes come true, and each charm gave her a special power. Tonight, she was flying thanks to the magic of her bird charm.

Stella caught hold of Cassie's hands and spun her round. 'Now you have all your charms,' she said, 'you're a Lucky Star. Just like me!'

'And now I can make anyone's wish come true?' asked Cassie.

'Of course!' Stella said. 'And I can show you more secrets of the Starry Sky. Let's go!'

They sped through the night, past tiny violet, orange and pink stars. Cassie thought she'd never get used to the brilliant colours of the stars, or how they played together, bobbing and dancing and chasing each other.

'Where are we going?' she called.

Stella spun round so that she was flying backwards. 'There's something special I want to show you,' she said. 'It's called the Winter Star, and it's one of the most beautiful stars of all. It sparkles like shards of crystal.'

8

The Christmas Wish

On they flew, until Stella suddenly gasped, 'Oh no!'

Cassie looked at the star just ahead, which was giving out a weak white light. 'Is that it?' she asked. 'That star's not bright at all.' When she saw Stella's horrified face, she asked, 'Something's wrong, isn't it?'

Her friend nodded. 'Something's terribly wrong. If the Winter Star is dim, it means winter will be full of gloom.'

'Oh no!' cried Cassie. 'Christmas is only a week away. It will be awful if everyone has a gloomy time.

Can I do anything?' She thought for a moment, then brightened. 'I could make some Christmas wishes come true!'

Stella smiled. 'That would be lovely, Cassie. If you can spread some Christmas cheer, maybe the Winter Star will shine brightly again.'

As they started back for home, Stella added, 'Remember, though, that not every wish is granted through magic.'

They sped down towards Astral-on-Sea. Cassie could see tiny waves rippling over the sand and twinkling lights strung along the pier.

'Stella, look at the beautiful Christmas tree outside the Town Hall,' she said. 'It's too big to go inside!'

The Christmas Wish

They swooped onwards towards Cassie's hilltop home. It was called Starwatcher Towers, because part of it was an observatory where her father worked, studying stars and planets.

'Your house looks so Christmassy, all lit up,' said Stella as they circled the domed glass roof of Cassie's bedroom.

'Mum likes to

make things perfect for the guests,' Cassie said. The other part of Starwatcher Towers was a bed and breakfast.

Stella dropped a kiss on Cassie's forehead, wished her starry dreams and flew up into the sky.

Cassie took one last look down the hill at Astral-on-Sea. How could she spread Christmas cheer? Everywhere already looked set for a wonderful Christmas. What could make it better?

Suddenly she knew. Snow! What fun it would be, building snowmen and tobogganing and playing with snowballs!

Cassie lifted her wrist and concentrated hard on her newest charm, a star. It gave her the power to make any wish come true

and, in moments, the magic began. A cloud
of silvery sparkles danced over the bracelet
and soft, silent snowflakes swirled around
her.

Cassie flung out her arms and twirled
in the air, letting snowflakes fall on her
upturned
face.

Everybody will be so excited when they wake up to a white world, she thought. She floated down through the open panel in her glass ceiling, hung up her coat and pulled back her duvet.

Twinkle, her dear old cat, was curled up under the covers, with just his head poking out. She dropped a kiss on his sleepy black and white face and he purred contentedly.

The Christmas Wish

Cassie's last thought, before she fell asleep, was about all the Christmas cheer her snowfall would spread. 'I'm so happy, Twinkle,' she murmured as her eyes closed.

2
Holly

The next morning, snow was still falling, and Cassie was building a snow cat in the garden of Starwatcher Towers. Her best friend, Alex, was making a snow puppy.

'Mum said she's never seen so much snow at the seaside before,' said Alex. He and his parents used to be guests at the B & B, but they liked Astral-on-Sea so much they decided to move there.

Cassie smiled as she added a floppy

ear to the snow puppy.

'What are you looking so mysterious about?' Alex asked. Then he drew a sharp breath. 'Did *you* make it snow?'

She nodded. Alex was the only other person who knew about her bracelet and her magic. He'd even shared her adventures.

Cassie quickly explained about the problem of the Winter Star. 'I made it snow to spread some Christmas cheer so the Winter Star will shine bright again,' she told him.

'That's amazing!' Alex said. 'I thought precipitation – you know, the water cycle – was sort of magical in its own way, but to create all this snow using a charm . . . Wow!'

Cassie put the finishing touch to her snow cat – a dark pebble for its nose. 'Done!' she said. 'Isn't it cute?'

19

'Not as cute as my snow puppy,' said Alex.

The front door opened, and Cassie's dad came out, carrying his smallest telescope. Behind him was Alex's bouncy white puppy, Comet, who'd been keeping warm indoors with Twinkle.

'Great snow animals!' said Mr Cafferty. 'They're just like Twinkle and Comet – only quieter.' He looked down the hill towards town, then made a face.

'What's up, Dad?' asked Cassie.

The Christmas Wish

'I've ordered the part I need to mend my telescope,' he said, 'but I don't think the delivery van will get up the hill. The snow's too deep.'

Oops! Cassie thought. *That's my fault. I made it snow.*

Suddenly Comet barked. 'Yupp! Yupp!' He ran to the gate.

Cassie stood up to see what he'd heard. A man carrying a suitcase, and a girl of about Cassie's age, were trudging up the hill.

Mr Cafferty greeted them. 'You must be our new guests, Mr Marshall and Holly,' he said. 'Welcome to Starwatcher Towers. My wife will have hot drinks ready for you in a flash, I'm sure.'

'Thanks!' said Mr Marshall. 'I hope my car will be OK. We left it at the bottom of the hill. We couldn't get through the snow.'

Oh dear, Cassie thought. *My snow's caused bother for our new guests.*

She said hello to Holly, who asked, 'Is that your puppy?'

'No, Comet belongs to Alex,' said Cassie.

Holly crouched down, her red hair falling over her face. 'Here, boy!'

She made a fuss of Comet, who wriggled

and snuffled at her hand. 'You are lucky, Alex, to have a puppy of your very own,' Holly said. 'Isn't he, Dad?'

Mrs Cafferty appeared at the door just then. 'Come in, everyone,' she said. 'I've made a big pot of hot chocolate, and there are freshly baked cherry shortbreads.'

Lucky Stars

They all sat round the big table, while Mr Marshall explained that he and Holly had come to Astral-on-Sea for the weekend, especially for the town's Christmas Fair.

'Holly's spending Christmas Day with her mum,' he said, 'so this will be our own special celebration.'

Mrs Cafferty put down the chocolate pot. 'Oh dear,' she said. 'I have some bad news. The Christmas Fair has been cancelled, because of the heavy snowfall. The stallholders and funfair people can't get to Astral-on-Sea, because the roads are too bad.'

Cassie felt terrible when she saw Holly's face fall. *I should never have made it snow*, she thought. *I've ruined everything.*

She took her
mug to the
sink, and Alex
followed.

'You made the
snow come,'
he whispered.
'Can't you make
it go?'

Cassie shook her head. 'If the snow just
disappears, people will guess that it's magic.
No, it's here until it melts. Oh dear,' she
murmured, 'maybe I should find out what
people actually *do* want to wish for before I
make anything happen.'

Alex nodded. 'Nobody wished for snow,'
he said.

'Exactly,' said Cassie. 'And, rather than spreading Christmas cheer, I'm making people miserable!'

3
Off to Flashley Manor

'Cheer up, Cassie,' Alex whispered. 'We'll think of something to turn all that snow into fun.'

'Yupp! Yupp!'

They looked through the window. Comet was rolling in the snow, his tail wagging. Whenever a snowflake landed on his nose, he barked.

Holly came to see. 'He's so funny!' she said.

Cassie heard a soft mewing sound coming
from the hall. Twinkle! She went to see
what was up, and found him in his basket
by the radiator. She turned her bracelet
round and concentrated on the crescent-
moon charm. Her wrist tingled as sparkles
streamed from the bracelet to curl round
Twinkle. The magic was working! Now
Cassie could understand her cat.

'What's wrong?' she asked.

The Christmas Wish

Twinkle looked grumpy. 'Comet's stupid, playing in that chilly, wet snow,' he said. 'If he had any sense, he'd sit in the warm with me.'

Cassie tickled his ears. 'You silly thing. You're just worried he'll catch cold. He'll be fine – his fur coat is thick and cosy.'

'Humph!' said Twinkle. 'Let him get as wet as he wants, if it keeps him happy.'

That gave Cassie an idea. Comet was having fun. Alex had said they could turn the snow into fun . . . Maybe she could cheer Holly up after all! She darted into the kitchen. 'Holly! Alex! Let's go sledging!'

Holly's face lit up. 'That would be almost as much fun as the fair!'

Mr Cafferty went to the shed to find a sledge, and Comet scurried indoors. Mum wrapped him up in an old towel and patted him dry.

Comet sneezed. 'Oooshoooo!'

From the hall, Cassie heard a very quiet, 'Told you so.'

Mr Cafferty returned with not one, but

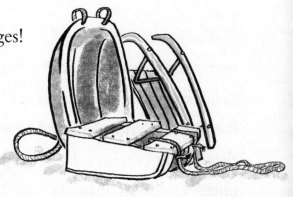

three old sledges!
Soon, Cassie,
Holly and
Alex were
bundled up
in coats,
boots, scarves and gloves, ready to go.

Mum said they were *not* to do any sledging on the road down into town. 'Use the hill behind Flashley Manor Hotel,' she said. 'It's safe there.'

They left Comet snuggled up with Twinkle, and set off with their sledges through the deep snow.

When Holly saw the Astral-on-Sea Christmas tree, she gasped. 'It's so beautiful.'

Lucky Stars

Cassie explained that everyone in town made decorations for the tree. 'Look,' she said, 'I painted those pine cones and put glitter on them. And see the roly-poly Santa Claus? The Mayor knitted that and stuffed it with old socks.'

'Look at my star,' said Alex. 'I used a cog and twelve lolly sticks.' He reached up, and showed her how the star's arms turned.

'That's so clever,' said Holly.

'Alex is mad about science and making things,' said Cassie. 'See the fairy? Our friend Kara from the fancy-dress shop made her outfit, and Farmer Greg sprayed those walnuts gold and hung them on red ribbons.'

'They're all fantastic,' said Holly. 'It looks so pretty.'

They plodded on, passing Bert, who in the summer ran donkey rides on the beach. He was taking a trailer-load of hay back to his stables.

'Must keep my donkeys warm and well fed,' he called.

When they reached the Fairy-cake Bakery, Cassie went inside and asked her friend Kate to come sledging with them.

'Love to,' said Kate. 'But first I must hang these on the Christmas tree.' She showed them a tray of gingerbread men that she'd iced in green and red, so they looked like Santa's elves. 'If there's time,

I'll catch up with you.'

'Invite any boys and girls you meet too,' said Cassie. She turned to Alex and whispered, 'See, we are spreading Christmas cheer!'

They reached Flashley Manor Hotel, and went past the huge front entrance to a smaller gate at the side. It opened on to a lovely snow-covered hill, just perfect for sledging.

Cassie pressed the handle, but it wouldn't move. 'It can't be locked,' she said. 'It's never locked.'

But it was.

She peered through the gate. 'Someone's sledging already,' she said. 'Guess who?'

'Donna Fox?' said Alex.

Cassie nodded. 'Donna's family run Flashley Manor,' she explained to Holly. 'She's really spoilt.'

'I can see that,' said Holly as Donna zoomed downhill, wearing a glitzy pink and gold ski jacket. 'That huge sledge must have cost a fortune.'

'It looks more like a sleigh,' said Alex.

Donna's brand-new sledge was also pink to match her ski jacket.

When she came
to a stop at the bottom of the hill, Donna
noticed Cassie and her friends. 'Come to
watch me, have you?' she sneered. 'Such a
shame you can't join in.'

Tossing her ponytail, Donna strode
uphill in her new snow boots. She stopped
halfway. 'Stay and watch if you want,' she
called, 'but I won't let you in. You'd never
go as fast as me anyway, not on those old

sledges. You'd just get in my way.'

Cassie glanced at Alex and Holly's disappointed faces. *Oh no*, she thought. *I can't even spread Christmas cheer to my friends. What sort of a Lucky Star am I?*

4
A Small Surprise

Donna zipped downhill again. 'See how fast my sledge is,' she shrieked. 'If you started off before me, I'd *still* beat you to the bottom!'

She punched the air with her fist. But as she did so the sledge swerved and shot into a dip. Donna shrieked, flew off and rolled over and over in the snow.

The sledge bounced down the hill and crashed into the gate.

Cassie, Alex and Holly jumped back in fright.

'Uh-oh,' said Alex. 'The front of her sledge has broken off.'

Donna stood up, brushing snow off her ski suit. She just scowled at first, but when she saw her sledge she turned bright red with fury! She stamped her feet. 'It's all your fault,' she snarled at Cassie and her friends. 'You distracted me! I'm going to tell my mum and dad!'

Cassie and Holly just stared, shocked at her outburst, but Alex crouched down to examine the sledge.

'I think I can fix it, Cassie,' he said. Then he yelled, 'Donna! I'll mend your sledge – if you let us in.'

Donna was silent for a moment, then she said, 'All right. But you'd better do it properly.'

Alex pulled string from his pocket, and unclipped his Do-It-All gadget from his belt. He was as good as his word, and in no time at all he stood up, saying, 'There you go. All fixed.'

'Brilliant, Alex,' whispered Cassie. 'Now she'll have to let us in.'

Donna sulkily unlocked the gate. She didn't speak, just turned away and pulled her sledge uphill.

Cassie grinned at Holly. 'Told you she was spoilt,' she said.

'Spoilt rotten,' agreed Holly. She took Cassie's hand. 'It was so nice of you to invite me sledging.'

'I'm glad you came, and I hope you have fun,' said Cassie. *I really do*, she thought. *I haven't spread much Christmas cheer so far.*

'Wait for me!' called Kate, running towards the gates carrying a sledge.

'I'm so glad you made it,' said Cassie. 'Kate, this is Holly. She's staying at Starwatcher Towers.'

'Hi, Holly!' said Kate. 'This is a great place for sledging. We're going to have loads of fun!'

Soon they were all whizzing down the slope, then laughing and joking together as they climbed back up. Donna carried on going up and down the hill, but she refused to join in any of the games.

'She couldn't have fun if she tried,' said Alex.

'Well, I'm definitely having fun,' laughed Holly as she climbed back on her sledge. 'Race you all!'

'You're on!' cried Cassie and Alex together.

When everyone was ready, Holly said, 'On your marks, get set . . .'

'Go!' shrieked Cassie. And she was off.

They shot downhill. Cassie felt so glad that her new friend was having a good time. *Looks like I've finally spread a little Christmas cheer*, she thought.

Near the bottom of the hill, she glanced around to see if she was in the lead, and completely lost her concentration. The sledge lurched sideways and slithered to a stop up against the thick hedge.

Phew! Cassie paused to get her breath back. Then her eye was caught by something moving, just inside the hedge.

'What's that?' she murmured, and got off her sledge to take a closer look.

It was a small animal – a bundle of white fur, with a little black nose.

'A puppy!' she whispered. She turned
to call to her friends. 'Alex! Holly! Kate!
There's a puppy here – just like Comet, but
even smaller!'

Everyone came closer, and Cassie picked
up the shivering little creature. 'You're so
cold,' she said. 'Here, let's wrap you up.'
She took off her woolly scarf and bundled
the puppy in it. 'There, you'll soon be
warm,' she said.

Holly gently stroked the puppy's head.
'I wonder who she belongs to,' she said.
'She's not wearing a collar.'

'I'll look around,' said Alex. 'Maybe I'll
see someone looking for her.' He trudged
over to the gate, just as Donna came to see
what was going on.

'What have you got there?' she demanded.

Cassie showed her. 'Isn't she adorable?' she said. 'We don't know who she belongs to.'

Donna paused for a moment, then said, 'It's mine.'

'Yours?' said Holly.

'Of course it's mine,' Donna snapped. 'It's right next to my hotel, isn't it? So it's mine. Obviously.' She held out her arms. 'Give it to me.'

Cassie was certain Donna was fibbing.
And I can't be sure she'd be kind to the puppy,
she thought. She glanced round as Alex
came back, shaking his head.

Donna saw her chance and dived for the
bundle in Cassie's arms. 'Give!' she said.

The puppy yelped, leapt free and
bounded off through the snow.

'Catch her!' cried Cassie. 'If she goes
right through the hedge, she'll end up on
the road!'

5
So Much Snow

'Let's spread out to search for the puppy,' said Alex. 'She'll be hard to spot, because white fur won't show up against the snow.'

Cassie crouched down to peer under the hedge. She crawled along, not caring that her knees were soaked, lifting the snow-laden branches for a better look. Finally, she saw something that *did* show up against the snow – a little, snuffling black nose!

'There she is!' she called. 'I'll have to get

right into the hedge to reach her, before she
runs into the road.'

Alex, Holly and Kate came to help, but
Donna stood well back. Cassie guessed she
didn't want to get her ski suit even wetter
than it was.

The four friends burrowed as far into
the hedge as they could. Cassie shivered as
snow plopped on the back of her neck, but
she knew that the puppy was even colder.
She could see her trembling miserably.

'Hurry up!' said Donna.

The puppy whimpered and shivered.
Cassie thought of what Twinkle had said.
This was no weather for a puppy to be
outside! But she couldn't reach her, and the
puppy wouldn't budge.

The Christmas Wish

Holly tried whistling. Kate tried snapping her fingers. Still the puppy wouldn't move.

'I wish we had some food,' said Alex. 'That always works when I have to get Comet out from under my bed.'

Aha, thought Cassie. *I can do something about that!*

She shook her bracelet free of her sleeve. The flower charm had the power to make things appear. She stared at it, concentrating like mad, and imagined there was a packet of Doggy Treats in her pocket.

Sparkles streamed from the charm and circled Cassie's wrist. She reached into her pocket and her fingers closed over a plastic wrapper. She pulled out a small packet of treats.

'Wow!' said Holly. 'Lucky you had those!'

'Er, Comet, um, treats . . .' Cassie mumbled, not wanting to fib.

Alex gave her a sly grin. 'Very lucky indeed,' he said.

Cassie knew Alex had guessed that she'd used her Lucky Star powers. She grinned back as she tipped a treat into her hand.

The Christmas Wish

'Hurry *up!*' said Donna. 'I'm cold.'

'Not as cold as the puppy,' muttered
Cassie. She held out her hand. 'Here, little
one.'

The puppy's nose twitched. A moment later, she crept forward until she was close enough to eat from Cassie's hand.

Alex reached out and gently took hold of her.

The four friends backed out of the hedge and shook snow off their heads and shoulders.

Alex gave the puppy to Cassie. 'Better wrap her in your scarf again,' he said.

'Can I feed her, please?' asked Holly.

Cassie passed her the bag, and soon the puppy was snuffling at the treats.

'Let's call her Snowdrop,' Holly said. 'It's a perfect name for something so small and lovely, found in the snow.'

Donna strode forward. 'I'll give it a name, not you,' she said, and tried to snatch the puppy.

But Cassie quickly turned away and headed for the gate. 'We're going to find out who Snowdrop belongs to,' she said. 'If she's really yours, ask your mum to come and fetch her.'

Donna's face was furious. She went bright red again, started stomping away – and slipped over, rolling all the way down the slope. When she got up again, she looked even more angry, and stamped towards the hotel.

'Mummy! Daddy!' she yelled. 'My ski suit's soaking wet. I need a new one and I need it NOW!'

Everyone said goodbye to Kate when they reached the Fairy-cake Bakery.

Cassie, Alex and Holly giggled as they walked towards Starwatcher Towers. It was hard pulling the sledges, because the snow was deeper than ever. Alex had to pull Cassie's as well, because she was carrying Snowdrop.

'I wish I was as tall as you two,' said Holly. The snow's nearly up to my knees! It's really hard going.'

'Sit on one of the sledges,' Cassie suggested. 'You can carry Snowdrop.' As Holly settled herself, Cassie turned aside and concentrated on her crescent moon charm. Sparkles swirled and whirled around the puppy.

The Christmas Wish

'Where do you live, little one?' Cassie whispered.

The puppy's tiny voice trembled as she answered. 'I haven't got a home. I can remember my mum, but I can't remember anything else.' She whimpered. 'I'm all alone.'

'You're not alone any more,' Cassie said comfortingly. 'We'll take care of you.'

She put Snowdrop in Holly's arms. Holly held Snowdrop close,

keeping her warm. 'You're so adorable,' she murmured.

Cassie smiled. She could see that Snowdrop was happy, even though the puppy couldn't understand what Holly was saying.

They set off again, with Alex pulling Holly and Snowdrop, and Cassie pulling the other two sledges.

As they neared the Town Hall, Alex said, 'The Christmas tree lights aren't shining as brightly as before. Must be the atmosphere.'

But Cassie soon realized what had happened. The tree's branches and lights were weighed down with snow. Too much snow. The tree looked top-heavy.

The Christmas Wish

As they gazed at it, the tree creaked.
It swayed. Then it creaked again, and
leaned to one side with a horrible groaning
noise.

'Cassie, get back!' Alex cried, pulling
Holly's sledge out of the way. 'The tree's
going to fall!'

6
A Shooting Star?

CRASH!

Cassie stared in horror as the Astral-on-Sea Christmas tree toppled to the ground, sending up clouds of snow.

Alex's mouth dropped open. Holly looked scared.

In the silence that followed, Cassie heard Snowdrop whimper. Then a voice cried, 'Oh no!'

She spun round to see the mayor run

out of the Town Hall. People came
out of shops and houses to see what the
commotion was.

'It wasn't our fault, Madam Mayor!' said
Cassie. 'I think the snow was too heavy
for the branches.' *My snow*, she thought
miserably.

'I was afraid that would happen,' said the

mayor. Snowflakes clung to her purple suit. She shook them off and sighed. 'Astral-on-Sea doesn't have enough money for a new tree. We'll have to have Christmas without it this year.'

The watching people groaned.

'But we always have a Christmas tree,' Cassie said in a small voice. 'Every year we sing carols around it.'

'Not this year, I'm afraid,' said the mayor. 'The snow has been too heavy.'

'Christmas won't be the same,' Cassie said sadly. She bent down and picked up one of Alex's star decorations. A lolly-stick arm had broken off.

She felt tears prickle her eyes. *This is all my fault for making it snow*, she thought. *How*

can I ever spread Christmas cheer now? I can't. I just can't.

Suddenly the mayor cried, 'There – a shooting star!'

Cassie looked up. A brilliant light was streaking across the snowy sky. She glanced at Alex. That wasn't a shooting star. It was Stella Starkeeper!

The light hovered over Starwatcher Towers for a moment, then burst into a glorious shower of silver sparkles.

The Christmas Wish

'It must have been a firework,' said Holly.

'A beautiful rocket,' said the mayor. 'I wonder who sent that up. And why . . .'

I know why, Cassie thought. *Stella's sending me a message. She's telling me not to give up.*

Cassie remembered what Stella had said: 'Remember . . . not every wish is granted through magic . . .' *That's where I went wrong by granting the snow wish,* Cassie thought. She looked around at her friends and at the fallen tree. Suddenly she knew exactly what Christmas wishes she must make come true – and she wouldn't need magic to do it.

A wonderful Christmas Fair for everyone in Astral-on-Sea, she thought. *A new Christmas tree in time for the carol-singing – and a home for Snowdrop.*

Cassie had a feeling that if she could just make those three wishes come true she'd spread enough Christmas cheer for the Winter Star to shine brightly once more!

She turned to Holly and Alex. 'I've got a plan!' she said. 'But first we've got to collect up all the tree decorations. Come on!'

7
Fun For All

The snow finally stopped falling in the middle of the afternoon.

Cassie looked around the garden of Starwatcher Towers. Fairy lights twinkled among the trees and on every bush, and decorations from the fallen Christmas tree adorned each branch. All the tables from the B & B were now Christmas stalls.

Cassie and Alex had asked lots of friends if they'd like to take part in the Starwatcher

The Christmas Wish

Towers Christmas fair. Everyone had said yes!

Farmer Greg arrived first, on his tractor. 'I've brought twelve jars of home-made plum chutney to sell,' he said, 'and some honey from my own bees. Oh, and I've used my tractor to clear the snow from the hill, so people can reach Starwatcher Towers easily.'

Soon the fair was crowded with people enjoying the stalls. Kate's mum sold warm mince pies from the Fairy-cake Bakery and Kate herself ran a guess-how-many-chocolate-baubles-are-in-the-jar game.

Kara arrived wearing a Christmas-pudding hat over her spiky pink hair. 'I've brought boxes of accessories,' she said.

'Scarves, hats, bracelets and red-and-green striped socks – I thought they looked Christmassy.'

Cassie hugged Kara, and introduced her new friend. 'Holly's helped me and Alex set up the fair. So did her dad, and Alex's parents, of course.'

'Great!' said Kara. 'Perhaps you could help me unpack my boxes!' As they did, she whispered, 'Why don't you two girls help yourself to something from my stall? It's a reward for organizing the fair for the town.'

Holly grinned. 'Thanks!' She took a silver bangle. 'It's not as lovely as your bracelet,' she said to Cassie, 'but it will remind me of you when I go home. What will you choose?'

Cassie hesitated, thinking, *I don't deserve a free gift*.

But Kara insisted. She held up a silver scarf. 'What about this?'

Cassie let the silky fabric slide through her fingers. She smiled. 'That's perfect, Kara. Thanks!' She folded the scarf carefully, and slipped it into her pocket.

A sudden 'Errrgh-hee-errrgh-hee-errrgh!' came from behind.

Cassie turned. 'It's Bert with three of his donkeys!' she cried.

'I saw you earlier with three sledges,' said Bert. 'If we hitch them to my donkeys, they can give rides to children.'

'Great idea!' said Alex. 'I'll harness the sledges for you.'

Cassie had an idea, too. 'Kara, have you any pairs of reindeer antlers?' she asked.

'Yes, three,' said Kara.

'Can we borrow them for an hour or so?' Cassie pleaded.

Kara nodded. 'Of course.'

Cassie got Alex to fix the antlers to the donkeys' bridles. 'There,' she said. 'Now

the children can imagine their sledges are being pulled by Santa's reindeers!'

Holly nudged Cassie. Donna Fox had arrived with her parents. They'd brought piles of home-made biscuits, and lemon tarts made from fruit grown in their conservatory.

'I hope the lemons aren't as sour as Donna's face was when she couldn't have Snowdrop,' Holly whispered.

Cassie laughed. They thanked the Fox family, then explored the rest of the stalls.

Alex's mum was doing a roaring trade, selling mugs of hot chocolate topped with cream and marshmallows. Cassie's dad sold hot baked potatoes oozing with melted butter, and Mr Marshall was roasting chestnuts. The delicious smells made everyone feel hungry.

Towards the end of the afternoon, the sky darkened. The fairy lights twinkled even more brightly, and there was a happy buzz of laughter and chatter.

The mayor clambered carefully on to a bench and clapped her hands for quiet. 'I have an announcement,' she said. 'We've had a quick count, and the good news is that the Starwatcher Towers Fair has raised more than enough money to buy a new Christmas tree for Astral-on-Sea. It's been a wonderful afternoon and everyone's had lots of fun!' She looked round, beaming. 'Thank you, Cassie, Alex and Holly – and well done, everybody!'

Mr Cafferty helped the mayor down, then Alex tugged at her sleeve. He held a clipboard with a long list of names on it. Cassie noticed they were all crossed out except one.

'We found a little white puppy today,' Alex said to the mayor. 'I'm trying to find her owner.' He tapped his clipboard. 'You're the last name on the list. Does the puppy belong to you?'

'Sorry, no,' said the mayor.

Alex turned to Cassie. 'That concludes my survey,' he said. 'Snowdrop is definitely a stray.'

Cassie felt sad. 'Poor puppy,' she said. 'Let's go and see her.'

In the kitchen they found the Caffertys

chatting with Alex's parents and Mr Marshall. Holly was playing on the floor with Snowdrop and Comet, while Twinkle watched from his basket.

'Alex did a survey,' said Cassie. 'He discovered that Snowdrop has no owner, and no home to go to.'

'In that case,' Mr Marshall said, 'I would like to offer Snowdrop a home with Holly and me.'

Holly leapt up and threw her arms round her father, squealing with delight. 'Thank you, Dad, thank you!' she cried. 'I've always wished for a puppy of my very own. Now my wish has come true!' Holly picked up Snowdrop and gave him a cuddle.

That night, Cassie sat in bed, stroking
Twinkle, and thinking about the snowy
day.

She got up, fetched her coat and slipped
it on over her pyjamas. Then she opened a
glass panel in her ceiling, and stood on her
bed.

Cassie looked at her bracelet,
concentrating hard on the bird charm. Her
wrist tingled and sparkles swirled all around
her.

Whispering goodbye to Twinkle, she
rose off the bed and floated up into the
night. The snow clouds had cleared, and
the sky sparkled with twinkling stars.

Cassie patted her pocket. Tucked inside
was the silver scarf from Kara's stall. Now

it was wrapped in purple paper dotted with
glittery stars.

*The scarf will go perfectly with Stella's silver
clothes*, Cassie thought.

As she flew through the sky, she saw a
bright light shooting towards her.

'Stella Starkeeper!' Cassie cried.

Her friend flew to hug her. 'Cassie, my
Lucky Star,' she cried, her velvety-blue
eyes shining. 'I'm so proud of you! You
made the whole town's Christmas wishes
come true,' she said, 'and not just with your
magical powers. Your determination made
things happen, as well.'

'I remembered you saying that not every
wish is granted by magic,' said Cassie. 'And
I've learned something important. I must be

sure of what people are really wishing for, rather than just guessing.'

'Your snow wish didn't work out, then?' Stella said, smiling.

'Definitely not!' said Cassie. 'And, Stella, thanks to you, I've also learned to never, ever give up.'

Stella took her hands and they whirled around together. 'You have lots more to discover and learn,' she said, 'and many more adventures to come.'

Cassie felt so happy she turned head over heels. Then she remembered the present in her pocket. She took it out. 'This is for you,' she said.

Stella opened the parcel and looped the scarf round her neck. 'It's gorgeous, Cassie!'

she cried. 'Thank you so much. It will go with everything I wear!'

Just then, over Stella's shoulder, Cassie noticed an unusually bright star. It glowed and sparkled with a light like silvery-white frost.

'Look at that,' she breathed.

Stella turned to see. She gave Cassie a warm smile. 'That's the Winter Star,' she said. 'It's shining again. Thanks to you, everyone will have a wonderful winter and a happy Christmas, full of cheer.'

They hugged goodbye, and Cassie flew back down to Starwatcher Towers, feeling perfectly content. As she floated down through the glass ceiling to her cosy bed, she thought she heard Stella's soft voice call, 'Good night, Cassie. Starry dreams!'

'Good night, Stella,' she murmured sleepily. 'See you very soon.'

Cassie's Things to Make and Do!

Join in the Lucky Stars fun!

Christmas Crossword

I love puzzles! Why don't you make a cup of hot chocolate and then see if you can answer my Christmas crossword?

Across

3. What did Kate and her mum bring to the Christmas Fair? (5,4)

4. What did I make shine brightly with the Christmas cheer I spread? (6, 4)

5. What animals gave rides at the Christmas Fair? (7)

Down

1. What did we call the puppy we found? (8)

2. What Christmas present did I give to Stella Starkeeper? (5)

6. What fun activity did me, Alex, Holly, Kate and Donna do in the snow? (8)

Kate's Mince Pies

Kate and her mum make the most delicious mince pies at the Fairy-cake Bakery! They gave me a copy of the recipe so Mum and I can bake them for all the guests at Starwatcher Towers. Why don't you make some yummy pies too?

Ingredients

125g unsalted butter, diced

225g plain flour

2 tablespoons caster sugar

pinch of salt

1 large egg, beaten

350g mincemeat

milk or a beaten egg for glazing

How to make

1. Preheat the oven to 200°C or gas mark 6. Ask an adult to help you with this!

2. Use some butter or oil to grease a twelve-hole baking tray.

3. Rub together the diced butter and flour in a bowl, and then add the caster sugar and a pinch of salt. Add the egg to the bowl and mix together.

4. Roll out the pastry thinly and cut into twelve circles, large enough to fill the holes in the tray. (Make sure to leave some pastry for the lids!)

5. Places the circles of pastry on to the baking tray and, using a spoon, fill each one with the mincemeat.

6. Cut twelve smaller circles (or you could make star shapes!) and place on top of the mincemeat.

7. Brush the tops with milk, or a beaten egg, and make a small hole in the top of each lid.

8. Ask an adult to help you place the tray in the oven. After around twenty minutes your mince pies will be ready – they should have turned golden brown. Put them on a wire tray to cool. Then eat!

Make your own snowflake decorations!

You can have a snowy Christmas, just like we did in Astral-on-Sea! These snowflake decorations are very easy to make, but you might need to ask an adult to help you with the cutting.

All you will need is

★ White paper circles (use the bottom of a cup or a small plate as a guide, depending on the size you want)

★ Scissors

★ Cotton

How to make

1. Draw a circle on a piece of white paper.

2. Cut out, then fold the circle in half and then in half again to make a curved triangle shape.

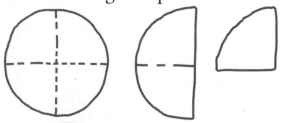

Cassie's Top Tip:
Try folding the paper in different ways to create patterns. You can also use coloured paper, or decorate with glitter, sequins or brightly coloured patterns – making them extra special!

3. Cut shapes into the sides of the paper (all three sides, but be careful not to cut all the way across the paper), using the scissors.

4. Unfold the paper and you will have your own, unique snowflake!

5. Make a small hole at the top of your snowflake decoration (ask a grown-up to help you with this) and then thread some cotton through and tie it in a knot, making a loop. Now you can hang it from your

Christmas tree, or
anywhere else
that needs some
Christmas cheer!

Christmas Crossword

```
        ¹S                              ²S
³M  I  N  C  E  P  I  E  S              C
        O                               A
        ⁴W  I  N  T  E  R  S  T  A  R   R
        D                               F
        R
        ⁵D  O  N  K  E  Y  ⁶S
        P              L
                       E
                       D
                       G
                       I
                       N
                       G
```

Answers

Don't look unless
you're really stuck!

Lucky Stars
Wishes really do come true

While Cassie was training to be a Lucky Star, she made lots of new friends. You'll meet them all too in the Lucky Stars stories!

Cassie

Alex

Comet

Twinkle

Stella

Sita

Sunbeam

Jacey

Holly

Marcus

Roxy

Snowdrop

Izzy

The Best Friend Wish

Phoebe Bright

With a whizz, fizz
and pop, magical Stella
Starkeeper appears and tells
Cassie she will be a Lucky Star –
someone who can grant wishes.
Could Alex, her new friend,
have a secret wish?

The Perfect Pony Wish

Phoebe Bright

Sunbeam the pony has
run away! Cassie must help
a little girl's wish come true and
find him before the showjumping
competition begins. Will
Sunbeam be the perfect pony?

The Pop Singer Wish
Phoebe Bright

Pop sensation
Jacey Day is performing
in Astral-on-Sea, but her
backing singers are ill! Jacey
wishes someone could fix things . . .
Cassie must find a way for
the show to go on!

Wishes really do come true...

Lucky Stars

The Birthday Wish

Phoebe Bright

Lia has a cake
disaster at her party!
What this birthday really needs
is a sprinkling of Lucky Star magic . . .
Can Cassie make a special
birthday wish come true?

Wishes really do come true...
Lucky Stars

The Film Star Wish

Phoebe Bright

Cassie makes friends
with Roxy Gold, film star!
Being famous is fun, but sometimes
Roxy wishes she could be
invisible for a day . . .

Wishes really do come true...
Lucky Stars

The Ballerina Wish

Phoebe Bright

Izzy is dancing the
lead role in Cinderella, but
she wishes she could remember
the steps! Can Cassie help her to
become the perfect princess?

Wishes really do come true

Lucky Stars

Look out for more magical Lucky Stars
adventures with Cassie and her friends!

The Sleepover Wish
Out in February 2013

The Ice Skating Wish
Out in February 2013

The Swimming Gala Wish
Out in April 2013

Wishes really do come true

Lucky Stars

Explore the magical world
of Lucky Stars!

For fun things to make and do – as well
as games and quizzes – go to:

www.luckystarsbooks.co.uk

Cassie is training to become a Lucky Star –
someone who can make wishes come true!
Follow her on more exciting adventures as
she meets new friends in need of help.

www.luckystarsbooks.co.uk